The Absent-Minded
Professor's
Memory Book

The Absent-Minded Professor's
Memory Book

Michele Slung

Illustrations by Jan Drews

Ballantine Books

Grateful acknowledgment is made for permission to use previously published material from
the following:

A Dictionary of Mnemonics (London: Eyre Methuen, 1972) Copyright © 1972 by Eyre
    Methuen. (*Meanings of the Stem "Mal."* E. E. Wallwork; *Latin Verb Formations*, Jacob C.
    Thompson; *Common French Adjectives*, Arnold Reuben; *French Nouns Ending in "ou,"*
    Arnold Reuben; *The Difference Between Bactrian and Dromedary*, Mark Palmer; *Vitamins*,
    E. J. Bowen; *Treatment for Stings*, Mrs. Peter More.)
The Elementary School Journal. Vol. XLV, No. 4 (Dec. 1944), "Simple Memory Devices for the
    Classroom" by Julian M. Scherr. Copyright 1944 by the University of Chicago Press. (*A
    Nutshell History of the American Revolution; Spelling Manhattan.*)
Pronouncing Author's Names. Copyright © 1980 by William Cole.
Irving's Anatomy Mnemonics by Alastair G. Smith (4th ed., published by Churchill
    Livingstone). Copyright © 1975 by Longman Group Limited. (*Layers of the Scalp; Course
    of the Oculomotor Nerve; Path of the Facial Nerve in the Facial Canal.*)

Library of Congress Catalog Card Number: 84-91668

ISBN: 0-345-31777-7

Text design by Ann Gold
Cover design by Herbert Pretel
Manufactured in the United States of America

First Edition: June 1985

10 9 8 7 6 5 4 3 2 1

To those whose memories are poor
  Mnemonic dodges help ensure.
        —James Copner, *Memoranda Mnemonica*, 1893

For Rick

Acknowledgments

Andrew Abramowitz, Peter Berkjord, E. J. Bowen, Maurice Braddell, Benjamin C. Bradlee, Colin Brooks, Amanda Burden, Lawrence Cabot, Peter Caws, Gunnery Sgt. Corty Cortez (USMC), Marcus Cunliffe, Suzanne Curley, Sen. John Danforth, Sally Danforth, Wayne Deer, Timothy Dickinson, Bathilde Dopfler, Susan Dooley, Victor Emmanuel, Alice Fox, Eugene Fidell, Captain Jay Farrar (USMC), Betty Goss, Russ Gould, James Grady, Joan Heidemann, Lt. Cmdr. A. J. Hindle (USCG), Bill Hogan, Barbara Howson, Susan Isaacs, Pat Jacobberger, Jim Karepin, Gary Kenton, Marty Kaplan, Nina King, Mary Etta Knapp, Charles Krauthammer, Wendy Law-Yone, Bobbie Ann Mason, Joel Makower, Major Donald Maple (USA), Patricia McGerr, Eleni Meleagru, Gardner McFall, Mrs. Peter More, Laszlo Morocz, P. J. O'Rourke, Mark Palmer, Phyllis Palmer, Arnold Reuben, George Rickley, Maralee Schwartz, Louis Sheaffer, Howard Simons, Caron Smith, Philip Stevens, Scott Stone, Joan Tapper, Jacob C. Thompson, Peggy and John Thomson, Judith Van Ingen, Richard Waldhorn, M.D., F. E. Wallwork, Brigitte Weeks, Virginia Weinland, Janet Wray.

Contents

History   3
Geography   17
Religion   23
Language   29
Music   41
Food   43
Numbers   47
Science and Technology   51
Time   57
Plants and Animals   61
Anatomy and Medicine   65
Marine Navigation   71
Aviation   75
Military   79
Folk Wisdom   83
Weather   87
Miscellaneous   91

The Absent-Minded Professor's Memory Book

History

The Presidents of the United States

Georgie, Adams, Jeff, and Mad,
    James Monroe, John Quincy Ad,
Andy Jack and M. Van B.,
    William Hen, Ty, Polk, Z. T.
Mill Fill and Pierce, Buch and Abe,
    Johnson, Grant, Rutherford Hayes.
Garfield, Chet, next Grover C.,
    Before and after Harrison, B.
McKin, T. R., W. H. Taft,
    Wilson, Harding, Cal—no laugh.
Herbert Hoover, FDR,
    Harry Truman, Eisenhower.
Kennedy and LBJ,
    Dick, Ford, Jimmy, and Ron Rea.

George Washington, John Adams, Thomas Jefferson, James Madison, James Monroe, John Quincy Adams, Andrew Jackson, Martin Van Buren, William Henry Harrison, John Tyler, James Knox Polk, Zachary Taylor, Millard Fillmore, Franklin Pierce, James Buchanan, Abraham Lincoln, Andrew Johnson, Ulysses S. Grant, Rutherford B. Hayes, James A. Garfield, Chester A. Arthur, Grover Cleveland, Benjamin Harrison (Grover Cleveland), William McKinley, Theodore Roosevelt, William Howard Taft, Woodrow Wilson, Warren G. Harding, Calvin Coolidge, Herbert Hoover, Franklin Delano Roosevelt, Harry S Truman, Dwight D. Eisenhower, John Fitzgerald Kennedy, Lyndon Baines Johnson, Richard M. Nixon, Gerald R. Ford, Jimmy Carter, Ronald W. Reagan.

3

The First Twenty-One Presidents

First stands the lofty *Washington*,
That noble, great immortal one.
The elder *Adams* next we see,
And *Jefferson* comes number three.
The fourth is *Madison*, you know,
The fifth one on the list, *Monroe*.
The sixth an *Adams* comes again,
And *Jackson* seventh in the train.
Van Buren eighth upon the line,
And *Harrison* counts number nine.
The tenth is *Tyler*, in his turn,
And *Polk*, the eleventh, as we learn.
The twelfth is *Taylor* that appears,
The thirteenth *Fillmore* fills his years.
Then *Pierce* comes fourteenth into view;
Buchanan is the fifteenth due.
Now *Lincoln* comes two terms to fill,
But God o'errules the people's will,
And *Johnson* fills the appointed time
Cut short by an assassin's crime.
Next *Grant* assumes the lofty seat,
The man who never knew defeat.
Two terms to him; then *Hayes* succeeds,
And quietly the nation leads.
Garfield comes next, the people's choice;
But soon ascends a mourning voice
From every hamlet in the land.
A brutal wretch with murderous hand
Strikes low the country's chosen chief,
And anxious millions, plunged in grief,

U.S. HISTORY

Implore in vain Almighty aid
That Death's stern hand might still be stayed.
Arthur's term was then begun,
Which made the number twenty-one.

Continued to the fortieth president

Followed by *Cleveland*, one of two times,
Then *Harrison* to the White House climbs.
Cleveland again, next *McKinley*, who's killed;
T. R., twice in, as Rough Rider is billed.
Come we to *Taft* and *Wilson's* eight years;
The twenty-ninth president, *Harding*, one fears
Will taint the office with Teapot Dome,
But *Coolidge* succeeds and makes it his home.
A full term to him, he's followed by *Hoover*;
As presidents go, not much of a mover.
But next comes a shaker, old *FDR*—
Nearly four terms, including a war,
Are given to him before he dies
And *Truman* ascends to rule and be wise.
Elected once, too, he makes way for *Ike*,
Our thirty-fourth pres, whom almost all like.
Two terms to him, then JFK
Brings Camelot and new cachet.
Until in Dallas, one fateful day,
Shots are fired: we swear in *LBJ*.
(A lone assassin or was it a plot?)
Lyndon runs once, then does not.
Watergate undoes *Nixon*, forced to resign;
In his second term, *Ford* completes Dick's time.
Jimmy Carter comes in grinning,
But *Ronald Reagan* next does the winning.

The Fourteenth President

Franklin Pierce = Fourteenth President

The Kings and Queens of England

[Beginning with the House of Normandy]

Willie, Willie, Harry, Stee,
Harry, Dick, John, Harry Three,
One, Two, Three Neds, Richard Two,
Harry Four, Five, Six. Then who?
Edward Four, Five, Dick the Bad,
Harrys twain and Ned the Lad,
Mary, Bessie, James the Vain,
Charlie, Charlie, James again.
William and Mary, Anna Gloria,
Four Georges, William and Victoria.

Ned Seventh ruled til 1910,
When George the Fifth came in, and then
Ned Eight departed when love beckoned,
Leaving George Six and Liz the Second.

*William the Conqueror, William II, Henry I, Stephen, Henry II, Richard I,
John, Henry III, Edward I, Edward II, Edward III, Richard II, Henry IV,
Henry V, Henry VI, Edward IV, Edward V, Richard III, Henry VII, Henry
VIII, Edward VI, Mary I, Elizabeth I, James I, Charles I, Charles II, James
II, William III and Mary II, Anne, George I, George II, George III, George
IV, William IV, Victoria, Edward VII, George V, Edward VIII, George VI,
Elizabeth II.*

The Kings and Queens of England Through Victoria's Reign

First *William the Norman*,
    Then *William* his son;

KINGS OF ENGLAND

Henry, Stephen, and *Henry,*
  Then *Richard* and *John;*
Next *Henry the Third,*
  Edwards one, two, and *three,*
And again after *Richard*
  Three Henrys we see.
Two *Edwards,* third *Richard,*
  If rightly I guess;
Two *Henrys,* sixth *Edward,*
  Queen Mary, Queen Bess.
Then *Jamie* the Scotchman,
  Then *Charles* whom they slew,
Yet received after *Cromwell*
  Another *Charles* too.
Next *James the second*
  Ascended the throne;
Then good *William* and *Mary*
  Together came on.
Til, *Anne, Georges* four,
  And fourth *William* all past,
God sent *Queen Victoria:*
  May she long be the last!

The Six Wives of Henry the Eighth

Cat of A, Anne Bo, and Jane See,
Anne of Clee, Cat Ho, and Cat P:
These three Cats, two Annes and a Jane
Were attracted by Hal to their bane.

Catherine of Aragon, Anne Boleyn, Jane Seymour, Anne of Cleves, Catherine Howard, Catherine Parr.

The Fates of Henry the Eighth's Wives

> Divorced, beheaded, died;
> Divorced, beheaded, survived.

The Ruling Houses of England

> No Point Letting Your Trousers Slip Half-Way.
>
> *Norman, Plantagenet, Lancaster, York, Tudor, Stuart, Hanover, Windsor.*

Which Side Was Which in the Wars of the Roses?

> Think of White Plains, New York.
> —Mary Etta Knapp
>
> *White rose—emblem of House of York; red rose—emblem of House of Lancaster.*

The Original Thirteen States in the Order in Which They Joined the Union

> *Del, Penn, N.J.*
>   Led the way.
> *George, Conn, Mass—*
>   Next in class.
> Seven, *Mary;*
>   Eight, *South Carrie.*
> *New Hamp,* nine on
>   The founding slate.
> *Virginia,* ten;
>   *New York* was late.

N.C., R.I.,
    They cast the die
And saved the day
    For the U.S.A.

Delaware, Pennsylvania, New Jersey, Georgia, Connecticut, Massachusetts, Maryland, South Carolina, New Hampshire, Virginia, New York, North Carolina, Rhode Island.

A Nutshell History of the American Revolution

Think of the phrase:

LIBERTY, 1775–81
1775 . . . Lexington (Battle)
1776 . . . Independence (Declaration)
1777 . . . Burgoyne (Surrenders)
1778 . . . Evacuation (Philadelphia)
1779 . . . Richard (Bonhomme)
1780 . . . Treason (Benedict Arnold)
1781 . . . Yorktown (Battle and Treaty)
                    —Julian Scherr

The Confederate States

Ten friends were in an ark: two Carols, Ginny, Miss Flora, George, Tex, Al, and Lou, then who?

Tennessee, Arkansas, South Carolina, North Carolina, Virginia, Mississippi, Florida, Georgia, Texas, Alabama, Louisiana.

The Battle of Hastings

William the Conqueror, ten-sixty-six,
    Played on the Saxons oft-cruel tricks.

The Discovery of America

In fourteen hundred and ninety-two,
Columbus sailed the ocean blue.

The Defeat of the Spanish Armada

The Spanish Armada met its fate
In fifteen hundred and eighty-eight.

Guy Fawkes Day

[Commemorating the Plot against James I in 1605]

Please to remember
The fifth of November,
Gunpowder, treason, and plot:
This was the day the plot was contriv'd,
To blow up the king and Parliament alive.

The Decisive Battle of the English Civil War

In sixteen hundred and forty-four,
They fought the battle of Marston Moor.

The Great Fire of London

In sixteen hundred and sixty-six,
London burned like rotten sticks.

WAR OF THE ROSES

The Accession of George III/ Also, How Many Yards in a Mile

George the Third said with a smile,
'Seventeen-sixty yards in a mile.

This is an unusual double mnemonic in which the year George III gained the throne of England turns out to be the same as the number of yards in a mile.

The Beginning of the American Civil War

When the North the South did shun,
Twas eighteen hundred sixty-one.

The End of the American Civil War

When the union did survive,
Twas eighteen hundred sixty-five.

The Uniforms of the American Civil War

Blue = Union (North)
Gray = Confederacy (South)

The Difference Between the Roundheads and the Cavaliers

Roundheads followed Cromwell.
Cavaliers followed Charles I.

The Opposing Factions in the Russian Revolution

Bowl Me over.

The Bolsheviks suppressed the Mensheviks.

The Early Roman Kings

Romulus founded the city;
  Numa Pompilius then
Founded the Roman religion,
  Striving to elevate men.

Tullus Hostilius, warrior,
  Had a belligerent reign
With Ancus Marcius, ditto,
  The Latins contended in vain.

Tarquin the Elder, succeeding,
  Built the great circus and sewer;
Servius Tullius, needing
  A census, the same did procure.

But a prince soon after committed
  A crime that could not be allowed;
And the Roman monarchy ended
  By expelling Tarquin the Proud.

The Death of Charles II of France,*
known as Charles the Fat

Charles the Fat ate, ate, ate.

Charles II died in 888.

* As Holy Roman Emperor, he was Charles III.

Injustices Righted by the English Reform Bill of 1832

BURPS

Bribery, Unrepresentative, Rotten boroughs, Pocket boroughs, Sale of seats.

Geography

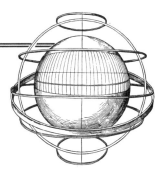

Remembering the Compass Points, Clockwise

Never Eat Shredded Wheat.

North, East, South, West

The Four Major Bodies of Water

PATINA

Pacific Ocean, ATlantic Ocean, INdian Ocean, Arctic Ocean.

The Great Lakes

HOMES

Huron, Ontario, Michigan, Erie, Superior.

The Seven Hills of Rome

Queen Victoria Can Eat Pie And Coffee.

or

MANHATTAN STREETS

Quiet Volcanoes Can Erupt, Puff, And Cool.

Quirinal, Viminal, Capitoline, Esquiline, Palatine, Aretine, Coelian.

New York City Numbered Streets

Eastbound streets are even.
  Westbound streets are odd.
Obey the traffic signals
  And leave the rest to God.

The Counties of Northern Ireland

Always A Dreadful Land For Trouble.

Antrim, Armagh, Down, Londonderry, Fermanagh, Tyrone.

The Train Stops on Philadelphia's Main Line

Old Maids Never Wed And Have Babies.

Overbrook, Merion, Narberth, Wynnewood, Ardmore, Haverford, Bryn Mawr.

The Capital of Alaska

Juneau [D'you know] the capital of Alaska?

Juneau.

The Capital of Idaho

Boys like Idaho.

Boise.

The Capital of Kansas

We like to peek at Kansas.

Topeka.

The Capital of Maine

There's a gust o' wind in Maine.

Augusta.

The Capital of Michigan

In Michigan the land sings.

Lansing.

The Capital of Montana

There's hell in Montana.

Helena.

The Capital of North Carolina

North Carolina, really?

Raleigh.

The Capital of South Dakota

We peer at South Dakota.

Pierre. (A reminder also to pronounce this as *pēr*.)

The Capital of Virginia

There's a <u>rich man</u> in Virginia.

Richmond.

The Capital of Wisconsin

I'm <u>mad at my son</u> in Wisconsin.

Madison.

The Capital of Wyoming

<u>Shy Ann</u>'s a bashful Wyoming cowgirl.

Cheyenne.

Religion

The Books of the Old Testament

> The great Jehovah speaks to us
> In *Genesis* and *Exodus*;
> *Leviticus* and *Numbers* see,
> Followed by *Deuteronomy*.
> *Joshua* and *Judges* sway the land,
> *Ruth* gleans a sheaf with trembling hand.
> *Samuel* and numerous *Kings* appear
> Whose *Chronicles* we wondering hear.
> *Ezra* and *Nehemiah* know
> *Esther* the beauteous mourner show.
> *Job* speaks in sighs, David in *Psalms*;
> The *Proverbs* teach to scatter alms.
> *Ecclesiastes* then comes on,
> And the sweet *Song of Solomon*.
> *Isaiah*, *Jeremiah*, then
> With *Lamentations* takes his pen.
> *Ezekiel*, *Daniel*, *Hosea*'s lyres
> Swell *Joel*, *Amos*, *Obadiah*'s.
> Next *Jonah*, *Micah*, *Nahum* come,
> And lofty *Habakkuk* finds room—
> While *Zephaniah*, *Haggai* calls,

Rapt *Zachariah* builds his walls.
And *Malachi*, with garments rent,
Concludes the ancient Testament.

The Pentateuch

G̲eorge's E̲vening L̲essons N̲ever D̲ull.

G̲enesis, E̲xodus, L̲eviticus, N̲umbers, D̲euteronomy.

The Books of the New Testament

Matthew, Mark, Luke, and *John* wrote the life of their Lord;
The *Acts*, what Apostles accomplished, record;
Rome, Corinth, Galatian, Ephesus hear
What *Philippians, Colossians, Thessalonians* revere:
Timothy, Titus, Philemon precede
The *Epistle* which Hebrews most gratefully read;
James, Peter, and *John*, with the short letter *Jude*,
The rounds of *Divine Revelation* conclude.

The Twelve Apostles

BAPTISM

*B̲artholomew, A̲ndrew, P̲eter/P̲hilip, T̲homas, I̲ = John/James/Jude/Judas,
S̲imon, M̲atthew.*
Here I̲ stands for J; these two were not treated as separate letters until
the nineteenth century.

The Rivers Out of Eden

The rivers that flowed out of Eden were these—
Pisón, Gihon, Hiddekel, and Euphratés.

The Nine Orders of Angels

Seraphim, Cherubim,
  Come take your *Throne.*
Dominions and *Virtues*—
  Their *Powers* alone.
Angels, Archangels,
  Next he sees,
Seated alongside
  Principalities.

The Ten Plagues of Egypt

Before Folks Let Flee Moses, Beastly Happenings Loosed
Dreadful Fears.

Blood, Frogs, Lice, Flies, Murrain (pestilence), Boils, Hail, Locusts, Darkness, First-born.

The Ten Commandments

Thou no God shalt have but me;
Before no idol bow the knee;
Take not the name of God in vain
Nor dare the Sabbath day profane;
Give both thy parents honor due;
Take heed that thou no murder do;
Abstain from words and deeds unclean
Nor steal, though thou art poor and mean;
Nor make a willful lie, nor love it.
What is thy neighbor's, do not covet.

TYPES OF ANGELS

The Seven Deadly Sins

PWELGAS

Pride, Wrath, Envy, Lust, Gluttony, Avarice, Sloth.

The Seven Virtues

For High Court Judge, Pity Tempers Force.

Faith, Hope, Charity, Justice, Prudence, Temperance, Fortitude.

The Principles of Calvinism

TULIP

Total depravity, Unconditional election, Limited atonement, Irresistible grace, Perseverance of saints.

The Four Types of Prayer in the Roman Catholic Church

ACTS

Adoration, Contrition, Thanksgiving, Supplication.

or

RAPT

Repentance, Adoration, Petition, Thanksgiving.

Language

The Parts of Speech

Three little words you often see
Are *articles*: a, an, and the.

A *noun*'s the name of anything—
As, garden or school, hoop or swing.

Adjectives tell the kind of noun—
As, great, small, pretty, white, or brown.

Instead of nouns the *pronouns* stand:
Her head, his face, your arm, his hand.

Verbs tell of something being done:
To read, count, sing, laugh, jump, or run.

How things are done the *adverbs* tell—
As, slowly, quickly, ill, or well.

Conjunctions join the words together—
As, men and women, wind or weather.

The *preposition* stands before
A noun—as, in or through a door.

The *interjection* shows surprise—
As, oh! how pretty! ah! how wise!

The whole are called nine parts of speech
Which reading, writing, speaking teach.

29

Poetic Meter

Tróchĕe tríps frŏm lóng tŏ shórt.
Frŏm lóng tŏ lóng, ĭn sólĕmn sórt.
Slów spóndée stálks; stróng fóot yét íll áblĕ
Évĕr tŏ cóme ŭp wĭth thĕ dáctўl trĭsýllăblĕ.
Ĭámbĭcs márch frŏm shórt tŏ lóng.
Wĭth ă léap ănd ă bóund thĕ swĭft ánăpĕsts thróng.

—S. T. Coleridge

Trochaic ˊ˘, spondaic ˊˊ, dactylic ˊ˘˘, iambic ˘ˊ, anapestic ˘˘ˊ.

Using *I* and *E*

I before *E*,
Except after *C*,
And when pronounced *A*,
As in neighbor and weigh.

Some exceptions: *either, leisure, foreign, sheik, heifer, seize, weird, protein, height.* Also: *Neither foreigners nor financiers forfeited their weird heights leisurely.*

Spelling *Separate*

There is a rat in separate.

or

Your pa's in separate.

Spelling *Harassment*

It has one r and two s's, the same as does "her ass."

MAN-HAT-TAN

Spelling *Mississippi*

Remember <u>Miss</u> <u>is</u> <u>sipping</u>.

Spelling *Manhattan*

A <u>man</u> had a <u>hat</u>,
And the <u>hat</u> was <u>tan</u>,
And that's the way
To spell <u>Manhattan</u>.

The Difference Between *Principal* and *Principle*

The princi<u>pal</u> <u>pal</u> of the princi<u>pal</u>
Is always <u>polite</u> on princi<u>ple</u>.

The Difference Between *Capital* and *Capitol*

Capitol with an <u>O</u> has a dome;
Capital with an <u>A</u> is its home.

The Capitol (building) is located in the capital (city).

Pronouncing Authors' Names

Say "pooch."
Then A. Quiller-Couch.
Then Joseph Wood Krutch.

Authenticity's the thing
With John Millington Synge.

He's as English as Dover sole—
He's Antony—believe me—Powell.

Who could get every joke of
Vladimir Nabokov?

Leave it at once, it's not a good house:
I see no books by P. G. Wodehouse.

—William Cole

The Difference Between *Stationery* and *Stationary*

For "stationery," think of one piece of paper.
For "stationary," think of something at rest.

The Difference Between *Francis* and *Frances*

Frances = Her
Francis = Him

The Difference between *Lama* and *Llama*

A llama's a beast.
  A lama's a man.
If it's spelled with two l's,
It needs two more legs to stand.

The Difference Between a *Barrister* and a *Solicitor*

The barrister dropped his briefs and became a solicitor.

The Difference Between *Slander* and *Libel*

Slander is said.
Libel: pencil lead.

How to Pronounce *Quay*

When by a quay,
Think of the sea.
And don't say "kay,"
Say "key."

A List of Latin Prepositions Taking the Ablative

A, ab, absque, coram, de,
Palam, clam, cum, ex, and e.
Sine, tenus, pro, and *prae.*
Add super, subter, sub, and in
When State not Motion 'tis they mean.

The Latin Declensions

Nights Grow Darker After August.

Nominative, Genitive, Dative, Ablative, Accusative.

The Meanings of the Latin Stem *Mal*

Malo—I would rather be
Malo—in an apple tree
Malo—than a wicked man
Malo—in adversity.

LATIN

Latin Verb Formation

Caesar was right, though rather cheeky,
in saying, *"Veni, Vidi, Vici."*
Any boy is wrong who thinks he
said, *"Venivi, Visi, Vinxi."*

The Common French (Nonreflexive) Verbs Conjugated with *Etre*

Mrs. D. D. Van Parmet

Monter, rester, sortir, Descendre, Devenir, Venir, aller, naître, Partir, arriver, retourner, mourir, entrer, tomber.

The French Verbs Not Requiring *Pas* in the Negative

COPS

Cesser, Oser, Pouvoir, Savoir.

The Common French Adjectives That Precede Nouns

Bon, mauvais, méchant, sot,
Grand, petit, vaste, haut,
Vilain, jeune, vieux, beau,
Ancien, long, joli, gros,
Digne, cher, saint, nouveau.

The French Nouns Ending in *-ou* That Take the Plural Ending *-oux*

Mes choux, mes bijoux,
Laissez vos joujoux,
Venez sur mes genoux!

Regardez ces mauvais petits garçons
Qui jettent des cailloux à ces pauvres hiboux!

The Seven French Conjunctions

Mais où est donc Ornicar?

Mais, ou, et, donc, or, ni, car.

FRENCH VERBS NOT REQUIRING *PAS*.

Music

Placing Notes Correctly on the Musical Staff

Every Good Boy Does Fine.

E, G, B, D, F (notes on the treble staff lines).

F A C E

Notes between the treble staff lines.

Good Boys Do Fine Always.

G, B, D, F, A (notes on the bass staff lines).

All Cows Eat Grass.

A, C, E, G (notes between the bass staff lines).

The Order of the Musical Mass

Kenneth Goes Courting Sweet Baby Alice.

Kyria, Gloria, Credo, Sanctus, Benedictus, Agnus Dei.

Food

When to Eat Oysters

Oysters "r" in season.

One can more safely eat oysters and other easily spoilable foods in the months containing an r in their name.

The Difference Between the Sweet Potato and the Yam

Between the sweet potato and the yam
Confusion reigns. But here I am
To tell you that the experts say
The yam's larger, sweeter, hooray!
But—easier—it's also said
The 'tater's yellower, the yam more red.

How to Eat Soup Correctly

As little fish swim out to sea,
   I spoon the broth away from me.

I SPOON MY SOUP AWAY FROM ME

The Correct Proportions of Vinaigrette Dressing

Three times the spoon with oil of Lucca crown,
And once with vinegar procured from Town.

Mix salad dressing in proportions of 3 parts oil to one part vinegar.

Numbers

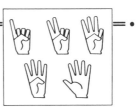

Roman Numerals

Let I make one
  And V stand five,
While X is ten,
  Then next arrive
At L for fifty,
  But on we drive.
C's a hundred,
  Followed by D
(It's five hundred,
  Or you tell me).
At last we come
  To M—a thou—
A largish figure,
  You'll allow.

The Order of Operations in Algebra

Please Excuse My Dear Aunt Sally.

Parenthesis, Exponents, Multiplication, Division, Addition, Subtraction.

CHIEF SOH·CAH·TOA

Pi (π) to Fourteen Decimal Places (3. 14159265358979)

3 · 1 4 1 5 9 2 6 5 3 5
Now, Dot, I find I still determine to suffer fools who laugh
8 9 7 9
whenever Grandpapa insults Grandmama.

The number of letters in each word reveals the decimal place.

The Trigonometric Functions

Chief *SOH-CAH-TOA.*

Sine = Opposite over Hypotenuse.
Cosine = Adjacent over Hypotenuse.
Tangent = Opposite over Adjacent.

Dividing Fractions

The number you're dividing by,
Turn upside down and multiply.

THE PHASES OF THE MOON

Science and Technology

The Order of the Planets from the Sun

Meek Violet Extraterrestrials Make Just Such Unusual New Pets.

Mercury, Venus, Earth, Mars, Jupiter, Saturn, Uranus, Neptune, Pluto.

The Phases of the Moon

When the moon doth make a C,
 It is decreasing hastily.
But when the C's reversed, please note:
 It's getting full and soon will bloat.

The Spectral Classification of Stars

Oh, Be A Fine Girl—Kiss Me Right Now, Sweetheart.

O (hottest), B, A, F, G, K, M, R, N, S (coolest).

The Colors of the Spectrum

Roy G. Biv

Red, orange, yellow, Green, Blue, indigo, violet.

or

The hues which form the rainbow's sheen
  In seven words are said—
Violet, indigo, blue, and green,
  Yellow, orange, red.

The Difference Between Stalactite and Stalagmite

Stalactite = ceiling
Stalagmite = ground

or

When the mites go up, the tights come down.

The Most Common Elements in the Human Body

P. COHN'S CAFE

Phosphorus, Carbon, Oxygen, Hydrogen, Nitrogen, Sulfur, Calcium (CA), Iron (FE).

The Periods of the Paleozoic Era

Cavemen Object Strenuously During Most Polite Parties.

Cambrian, Ordovician, Silurian, Devonian, Mississippian, Pennsylvanian, Permian.

The Periods of the Cenozoic Era

Pass Everything Over, Miss, Politely, Please, and Reasonably.

Paleocene, Eocene, Oligocene, Miocene, Pliocene, Pleistocene, and Recent.

STALAGTITES VS. STALAGMITES

Taxonomic Classification

Kings prefer crowns or fairly grand, similar vanities.

Kingdom, phylum, class, order, family, genus, species, variety.

The Order of Color Coding for First and Second Bands of Electrical Resistors (Values 0 Through 9)

Bad boys raped our young girls, but Violet goes willingly.

Black, brown, red, orange, yellow, green, blue, violet, gray,
 0   1   2   3   4   5   6   7   8
white
 9

Metric Measurement

Meters for length,
   Grams for weight,
Liters, capacity:
   The empty state.

The Shape of the Earth

Earth's diameter is greater
In the plane of the equator,
By miles no less than twenty-six
Than North and Southern Poles betwixt.

At the equator—7,926.4 miles; between the poles—7,899.9 miles.

WIDTH OF THE EARTH

The Seven Units of the International System (Weights and Measures)

Mere kisses seem ample; keep me cuddled.

Meter (length), kilogram (mass), second (time), ampere (electric current), kelvin (thermodynamic temperature), mole (amount of substance), candela (luminous intensity).

The Difference Between RAM and ROM (Computer Memories)

RAM (Random Access Memory) will record and play back:
  Think of a tape, which will do both.
ROM (Read Only Memory) can only play back:
  Think of a phonograph, which can only play back.

—Joel Makower

To Avoid Explosions in the Lab

PAW

Pour Acid (in) Water.
(Not the other way around.)

The Basic Metric Prefixes, in Descending Order

Kangaroos hop, dancing despite coming motherhood.

Kilo (thousandfold), hecto (hundredfold), deka (tenfold), deci (tenth part), centi (hundredth part), milli (thousandth part).

Time

The Days of the Months of the Year*

> Thirty days has September,
> April, June, and November.
> All the rest have thirty-one,
> Except the second month, we find,
> Has twenty-eight, til Leap Year gives it twenty-nine.

> *or*

> Thirty days hath September,
> April, June, and November.
> February has twenty-eight alone,
> All the rest have thirty-one,
> Excepting Leap Year—that's the time
> When February's days are twenty-nine.

> *or*

> Thirty days hath September,
> April, June, and November.
> All the rest have thirty-one,
> Excepting February alone.

* This is the oldest mnemonic device continually in use. One finds it written as early as the late sixteenth century.

SPRING FORWARD, FALL BACK

For three full years, remember, rate
February's days as twenty-eight;
But Leap Year coming once in four,
Adds to it always one day more.
A year that will by four divide,
To be a Leap Year we decide.

Setting the Clocks to Adjust to Daylight Saving Time

Spring forward; *fall* back.

Which Way the International Dateline Functions

When it's Sunday in San Francisco, it's Monday in Manila.

SAFE VS. POISONOUS SNAKES

Plants and
Animals

Evergreen Identification

Pines come in packages.
Firs are flat and flexible.
Spruce are square and stiff.

Wild Grass Identification

Sedges have edges, rushes are round.

Bear Cubs at Birth

Bears bear bare bears.

Newborn bears are hairless.

The Difference Between a Coral Snake (Poisonous) and a King Snake (Friendly)

Red and yellow,
Kill a fellow.
Red and black,
Friend of Jack.

CROCODILES VS. ALLIGATORS

HUMPS ON A CAMEL

Poison Ivy Warning

Leaflets three, let it be.

The Difference Between Alligators and Crocodiles

Now, a crocodile is hardly a runt,
But the alligator's snout is shorter and more blunt.
These two reptiles are of the same group—
If you meet them both at once, then you're in the soup.

The Difference Between Bactrian and Dromedary Camels— How Many Humps?

A camel I am, it's plain to see.
But am I a Bactrian or a Dromedary?
Lay down the ⊐ and then the ⊓,
And which I am is plain as can be.

Trees, Woody Plants, and Shrubs with Opposite Branching

MADCAP HORSE

*Maple, Ash, Dogwood, CAPrifoliaceae? [honeysuckle, viburnum, etc.],
HORSE chestnut.*

Putting Cut Flowers in Water

The harder the stem,
the hotter the water.

Anatomy and Medicine

The Bones of the Body

How many bones in the human face?
Fourteen, when they're all in place.

How many bones in the human head?
Eight, my child, as I've often said.

How many bones in the human ear?
Three in each and they help to hear.

How many bones in the human spine?
Twenty-six, like a climbing vine.

How many bones in the human chest?
Twenty-four ribs and two of the rest.

How many bones in the shoulder bind?
Two in each, one before and behind.

How many bones in the human arm?
In each one, two in each forearm.

How many bones in the human wrist?
Eight in each, if none are missed.

How many bones in the palm of the hand?
Five in each, with many a band.

How many bones in the fingers ten?
Twenty-eight, and by joints they bend.

How many bones in the human hip?
One in each, like a dish they dip.

How many bones in the human thigh?
One in each, and deep they lie.

How many bones in the human knees?
One in each, the kneepan, please.

How many bones from the leg to the knee?
Two in each, we can plainly see.

How many bones in the ankle strong?
Seven in each, but none are long.

How many bones in the ball of the foot?
Five in each, as the palms were put.

How many bones in the toes half a score?
Twenty-eight, and there are no more.

And now altogether these many bones fix,
And they count in the body two hundred and six.

And then we have the human mouth,
Of upper and under, thirty-two teeth.

And now then have a bone, I think,
That forms on a joint or to fill up a chink.

A sesamoid bone, or a wormian, we call;
And now we may rest, for we've told them all.

The Bones of the Wrist

Never Lower Tillie's Pants, Mama Might Come Home.

Naviculate, Lunate, Triangulate, Pisiform, Multangular/greater, Multangular/lesser, Capitate, Hamate.

The Twelve Cranial Nerves

On Old Olympus' Towering Top, A Finn And German Vault And Hop.

Olfactory, Optic, Oculomotor, Trochlear, Trigeminal, Facial, Auditory, Glossopharyngeal, Vagus, Accessory, Hypoglossal.

The Excretory Organs of the Body

SKILL

Skin, Kidneys, Intestines, Liver, Lungs.

The Layers of the Scalp

SCALP

Skin, Close connective tissue/cutaneous vessels and nerves, epicranial Aponeurosis, Loose connective tissue, Pericranium.

The Path of the Facial Nerve in the Facial Canal

Oh, Be Damned!

Outward, Backward, Downward.

The Course of the Oculomotor Nerve

Through peduncular cistern first I run,
Then pierce dura just for fun;
Here posterior clinoid is to medium
Between the two borders of tentorium.
Next laterally in the sinus I go,
Crossed by trochlear from below;

Into two branches then I split
And these round nasociliary fit.
Thro' orbital fissure next I pass
Between the heads of the lateral rectus,
Entering orbit that I may
Supply levator palpabrae.
Inferior oblique and recti three,
With twig to the ganglion come from me.

A Physician's Orders When Admitting a Patient to the Hospital

D. C. Van Dissel

Diagnosis, Condition, Vital signs, ambulation, nursing orders, Diet, intake and output, Symptomatic drugs, specific drugs, examinations, laboratory.

The Five Types of Wounds

A PAIL

Abrasion, Puncture, Avulsion, Incision, Laceration.

Vitamins

Vitamin A
Keeps the cold germs away
And tends to make people nervy.
B's what you need
When you're going to seed
And C is specific to scurvy.
Vitamin D makes the bones in your knee
Tough and hard for the service on Sunday.
While E makes hens scratch
And increases the hatch

And brings in more profits on Monday.
Vitamin F never bothers the chef,
For this vitamin never existed.
G puts the fight in the old appetite
And you eat all the foods that are listed.
So now when you dine, remember these lines,
If long on this globe you will tarry.
Just try to be good and pick out more food
From the orchard, the garden, and dairy.

Treatment for Stings

Ammonia—Bee stings
Vinegar—Wasp stings

In the alphabet, a is followed by b, v by w.

First Aid When Someone Has Stopped Breathing

A Quick Check.

A = Open airway passage
Quick = four *quick* breaths (adults), or
four *quick* puffs (children)
Check = *Check* pulse or breathing for spontaneous recovery, and
Check general appearance

First Aid Procedure for Noncorrosive Poison

FDR

Fill (give liquid to victim)
Drain (induce vomiting)
Refill (introduce more liquid into victim)

Marine Navigation

Heading into Shore in U.S. Waters (Lateral System)

Red right returning.

Keep red buoys on your right.

The Difference Between Port and Starboard

Port is *left*; both have four letters.

   or

Port light is *red*; port wine is *red*.

Compass Correction for True North and Magnetic North

Compass least,
  Error east.
Compass best,
  Error west.

PORT VS. STARBOARD

Compass Conversion for
True North and Magnetic North

Can Dead Men Vote Twice?

Compass reading, deviation, magnetic, variation, true

   or

Tender Virgins Make Dull Companions.

True, variation, magnetic, deviation, compass reading.

Buoyage

Even red nuns have odd green cans.

Tapered red buoys are even-numbered; cylindrical green buoys are odd-numbered.

Aviation

The Documents That Belong in an Airplane

ARROW

Air-worthiness certificate, Registration, Radio license, Operating limitations, Weight and balance forms.

Checklist Before Takeoff in a Propeller-Driven Airplane

CIGAR TIP

Controls (free?), Instruments (checked and set?), Gas (on main?), Altimeter (set?), Radio (set?), Trim (set for takeoff?), Ignition (both on?), Prop (full increase?)

Checklist Before Landing a Propeller-Driven Airplane

GUMP

Gas (boost pumps on?), Undercarriage (down?), Mixture (full rich?), Prop (full increase?)

LANDING/TAKE OFF

Finding Polaris (North Star) in Celestial Navigation

VEST

When Vega is East, Star is Top.

CELA

When Capella is East, draw Line Above to find star.

Military

The Marine Corps Basic Principles of War

MOOSE-MUSS

Mass, Objective, Offensive, Surprise, Economy of Offense, Movement, Unity of Command, Simplicity, Security.

Preparing a Five-Paragraph Tactical Order in the Marine Corps

BAMCIS

Begin planning, Arrange reconnaissance, Make reconnaissance, Complete planning, Issue order, Supervise.

The Marine Corps Five-Paragraph Tactical Order

SMEAC

Situation, Mission, Execution, Administration and logistics, Command and control.

The Marine Corps
Guidelines for Machine Gun Emplacement

COCOA

Cover, Observation, Concealment, Obstacles, Avenues of approach.

The Factors to Take into Account When Planning
a Tactical Operation in the U.S. Army

METT

Mission, Enemy, Troops, Terrain.

The Procedures to Orient the Firing of
U.S. Army Artillery Pieces

Take the fire out of the old lady.

Take the azimuth of fire out of the orienting line.

STARVE A FEVER

Folk
Wisdom

When Feeling Sick

> Feed a cold,
> Starve a fever.

> *or*

> Feed a cold, starve a fever;
> Eat 'tween sneezes so's to relieve her.

To Avoid Colds

> Colds "r" common—so don't sit on the grass in any month
> that has an "r" in it.

To Avoid Hangovers

> Beer on whiskey mighty risky,
> Whiskey on beer never fear.

Eating Garlic with Impunity

> If you munch a sprig of parsley,
> You needn't eat your garlic sparsely.

WHISKEY ON BEER

Cutting Thistles

Cut thistles in May,
   They grow in a day.
Cut them in June,
   That is too soon.
Cut them in July,
   Then they will die.

Early Harvest

Mist in May, heat in June—
   Make the harvest come right soon.

Weather

The Significance of the Wind's Direction

> When the wind is in the east,
> 'Tis neither good for man nor beast;
> When the wind is in the north,
> The skillful fisher goes not forth;
> When the wind is in the south,
> It blows the bait in the fishes' mouth;
> When the wind is in the west,
> Then 'tis at the very best.

> *and*

> The south wind brings wet weather,
> The north wind wet and cold together;
> The west wind always brings us rain,
> The east wind blows it back again.

Clouds Forecasting Rain

> When clouds appear like rocks and towers,
> The earth's refresh'd by frequent showers.

Rain, Forecast by a Pale Sunset

If the sun goes pale to bed,
'Twill rain tomorrow, it is said.

Imminent Rain, Forecast by the Moon

Ring around the moon:
    It'll rain soon.

Fair or Foul Weather, Forecast by the Sky

Red sky in the morning,
    Sailors, take warning.
Red sky at night,
    Sailors' delight.

or

The evening red, and the morning gray,
    Are the tokens of a bonny day.

Fair or Foul Weather, Forecast by Rainbows

Rainbow i' the morning,
Shippers' warning;
Rainbow at night,
Shippers' delight.

or

If there be a rainbow in the eve,
It will rain and leave.
But if there be a rainbow in the morrow,
It will neither lend nor borrow.

Fair Weather, Forecast by Wild Geese

If the wild geese head out to sea,
Good weather there will surely be.

How to Forecast Winter's Severity

Onion skin very thin:
  Mild winter coming in.
Onion skin thick and tough:
  Coming winter cold and rough.

Winter Advice for Pedestrians

Walk fast in snow,
  In frost walk slow,
And still as you go,
  Tread on your toe.
When frost and snow are both together,
  Sit by the fire and save shoe-leather.
                        —Jonathan Swift

Miscellaneous

Turning a Screw

Left loose, right tight.

or

A turn to the right makes it tight.

For Americans Driving in the British Isles

Think of "a well-dressed socialist"—look right, keep left.
—P. J. O'Rourke

British Titles in Order of Degree

Dignity Merits Each Very Big Bow.

Duke, Marquis, Earl, Viscount, Baron, Baronet.

Signs of the Zodiac, in Order

What are the signs of the Zodiac? Well,
Let *Aries, Taurus, Gemini* tell,

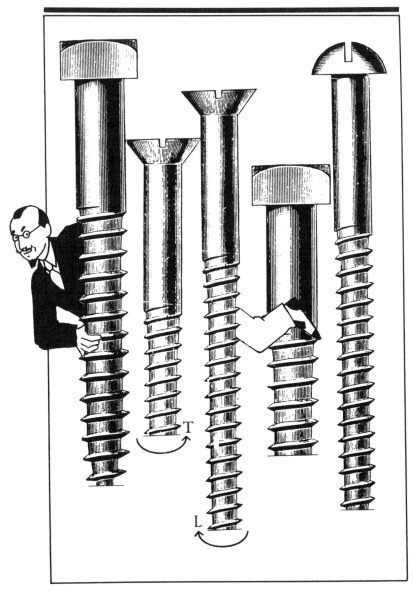

RIGHT-TIGHT/LEFT-LOOSE

Cancer, Leo, Virgo fair,
Libra, Scorpio, Sagittair,
Capricorn, Aquarius, and *Pisces* rare.
In memory fix these rhyming lines,
You'll know at once the Zodiac's signs.
Our vernal signs the *Ram* begins,

or

Then comes the *Bull,* in May the Twins;
The *Crab* in June, next *Leo* shines,
And *Virgo* ends the northern signs.
Then *Libra* brings autumnal fruits,
The *Scorpion* stings, the *Archer* shoots;
December's *Goat* brings winter's blast,
Aquarius *rain,* the *Fish* comes last.

Have you favorite ways of remembering facts to add to the *Absent-Minded Professor's* collection? If so, send them to

%
Michele Slung
Ballantine Books
201 East 50th Street
New York, New York 10022

Unfortunately, no compensation or credit can be given for your contributions.